ST. PROCOPIUS SCHOOL
1625 S. ALLPORT STREET
CHICAGO, IL 60608

The Berenstain Bears®
and the
BIG PICTURE

Stan & Jan Berenstain

A GOLDEN BOOK • NEW YORK

Western Publishing Company, Inc., Racine, Wisconsin 53404

Said Mama Bear,
"It seems to me,
you cubs watch
much too much TV!"

"Don't turn it off!
It isn't fair!"

"Don't turn it off!
Please, Mama Bear!"

"Watching all that
TV slush
will surely turn
your brains to mush.

"I will not argue.
I will not bicker.
I will keep
the TV clicker!"

"I beg you, Ma,
on bended knee.
Don't take away
our TV!"

But Ma was firm.
Ma was sure.
"This TV disease
has just one cure!"

The cubs were stunned.
The cubs were shocked.

Those TV-watching bears
were rocked!

Then Brother had a bright idea…
"Look out the window, Sister Bear.
I see another
world out there."

They opened up
the door a crack.
Now there was
no turning back.

When those TV bears
stepped outside,
their TV eyes
opened wide.

There were such amazing
things to see.
The cubs forgot
that old TV.

There was stuff called grass,

things called trees,

and flying things
called birds and bees.

15

And way, way,
away up high,

a big blue thing
called the sky.

There were other cubs
to run and play with,

and when they got tired—

to sit and stay with.

There were playground things
to climb and slide on,

and other things
to climb and ride on.

There was a thing called weather.
Sometimes it rained.

One day it even
hurricaned!

But then that thing
called sun came out
and spread its warmth
and light about.

Said Brother Bear,
"Who needs TV?"
Said Sister Bear,
"TV? Not me!"

"This other world
we have found
has a better picture
and better sound.

"And worlds of wonder
all around!

"Come! That thing up there
called the moon
means that we should
go home soon!"

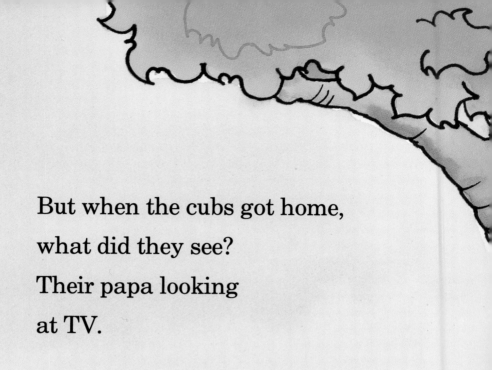

But when the cubs got home,
what did they see?
Their papa looking
at TV.

31

"Papa! Too much of
that TV slush
will surely turn
your brain to mush!"

ST. PROCOPIUS SCHOOL
1625 S. ALLPORT STREET
CHICAGO, IL 60608